HOW THE PATH GREW

By Poile Sengupta
Illustrated by Subir Roy

Children's Book Trust, New Delhi

In space
On earth
In the world
In Asia
In India
By a big hill
Was a little village called Yarala.

By the big hill
On the other side
Near a large railway-station
With big, big, trains
Was a huge town called Tathada.

In Yarala
In a house
With a garden
With mango trees
Lived a little girl called Sashaha
With her father and mother.

In Tathada
In a big building
With many rooms
With blackboards
With chalk
Was a school
Called Padhayi.

Every morning,
at eight o'clock
Out of her house
Out of her garden
Through the village
Over the hill
Through the town
To her school
Went the little girl
called Sashaha.

Every afternoon,
at four o'clock
Out of her school
Through the town
Over the hill
Through the village
To her house
Went the little girl
called Sashaha.

Between the huge town called Tathada
And the little village called Yarala
From the house
Through the village
Over the big hill
Through the town
To the school
Back through the town
Over the big hill
Back through the village
Back to the house
Grew a small path
Made by the little girl called Sashaha.

One day, in the village Yarala
In the house
Where lived the girl, Sashaha
In the garden
On the trees
The mangoes grew, big and golden.

Then the little girl, Sashaha
And her father and mother
Filled a cart
With the big, golden mangoes
From the trees
In the garden
Of the house
In the village called Yarala.

That morning, at eight o'clock
Out of the garden
Through the village
Over the hill
Through the town
To the market
Went the little girl, Sashaha
And her father and mother
In a cart
Filled with big, golden mangoes
And there they sold the mangoes.

That evening, at four o'clock
From the market
Through the town
Over the big hill
Through the village
Back to the house
Came the little girl, Sashaha
And her father and mother
In a cart
Filled with toys for Sashaha.

From the house
Through the village
Over the big hill
Through the town
To the market
Went the path
Made by the cart

In which sat the little girl, Sashaha
And her father and mother.

From the market
Through the town
Over the big hill
Through the village
Back to the house
Went the path
Made by the cart
In which sat the little girl, Sashaha
And her father and mother.
Everyday
The path
Made by the cart
Between the village, Yarala
And the town, Tathada
Grew bigger
And bigger
And bigger.

One day
In a big, big, train
To the railway-station
Near the town, Tathada
Came a clever man
Called Hahaho.

The clever man called Hahaho
Went in a car
Over the path
Made by the cart
Through the town
Up the hill...
And there the car stopped.

Because the path
Made by the cart
From the top of the hill
Down the other side
To the village
Was too small
For the car
In which sat
The clever man
Called Hahaho.

So the clever man, Hahaho
Had to push away bushes
And plants
And thorns
From the sides of the path
Made by the cart
To drive his car
From the top of the hill
Down the other side
Through the village
To the house
Where lived the little girl, Sashaha
With her father and mother.

The clever man, Hahaho
Ate many big, golden mangoes
From the trees
In the garden
Around the house
Where lived the little girl, Sashaha
With her father and mother.

And the clever man liked
The big, golden mangoes
And the clever man wanted
The big, golden mangoes
From the trees
In the garden
Around the house
In the village, Yarala
To be eaten by everybody
In India
In Asia
In the world
On earth
In space.

So the clever man, Hahaho
Filled with big, golden mangoes
Called many people
Called engineers
And they all made a wide road
From the railway-station
Near the town, Tathada
Through the town
Up the hill...

Down the other side
Through the village, Yarala
To the house
Where lived the little girl, Sashaha
With her father and mother.

And now
Between the village, Yarala
And the town, Tathada
Over the hill
Through the town
To the railway-station
Is a fine, wide road
With flowers
On both sides.

And in the middle of the road
Go cars and buses
And scooters and cycles
And a cart
Filled with big, golden mangoes
From the trees
In the garden
Around the house
Where lives the little girl, Sashaha
With her father and mother
In the village Yarala

In India
In Asia
In the world
On earth
In space.